Note to Parents

You are your child's first teacher.

You run alongside the training wheels as your child learns to ride a bike. You sit with an open book, encouraging him or her to sound out words, and you teach your child the importance of life-centering virtues.

Your child notices obedience when you stop at a red light, sees your patience while you wait at a store register, and enjoys the warm fuzzies of gratitude during the holidays. But merely exposing children to these concepts does not mean boys and girls will understand them.

As you read *Noah Builds a Boat*, be alert for opportunities to teach your child about the three virtues highlighted in this Bible story. For example, Noah was an obedient man. Even though people scoffed at this elderly gentleman's spending years hammering together a big boat, Noah did what God had asked. After sharing this part of the story, ask your child, "What does it mean to be obedient?" Or, after reading about the long rain, pause to talk about times when your child has been patient. And after finishing the story, thank your child for reading with you—perhaps he or she will thank you, too!

Dr. Mary Manz Simon

For Joshua John Pitney — MMS

To all the living creatures — LB

Text copyright © 2008 Mary Manz Simon. Illustrations copyright © Lyuba Bogan. All rights reserved. Published in the United States by Golden Books, an imprint of Random House Children's Books, a division of Random House, Inc., New York. Golden Books, A Golden Book, and the G colophon are registered trademarks of Random House, Inc.
Library of Congress Control Number: 2007920316
ISBN: 978-0-375-84250-4
www.goldenbooks.com   www.randomhouse.com/kids
PRINTED IN CHINA   10 9 8 7 6 5 4 3 2 1   First Edition

NOAH BUILDS A BOAT

A Story of Obedience, Patience, and Gratitude

by Dr. Mary Manz Simon
illustrated by Lyuba Bogan

A GOLDEN BOOK ◆ NEW YORK

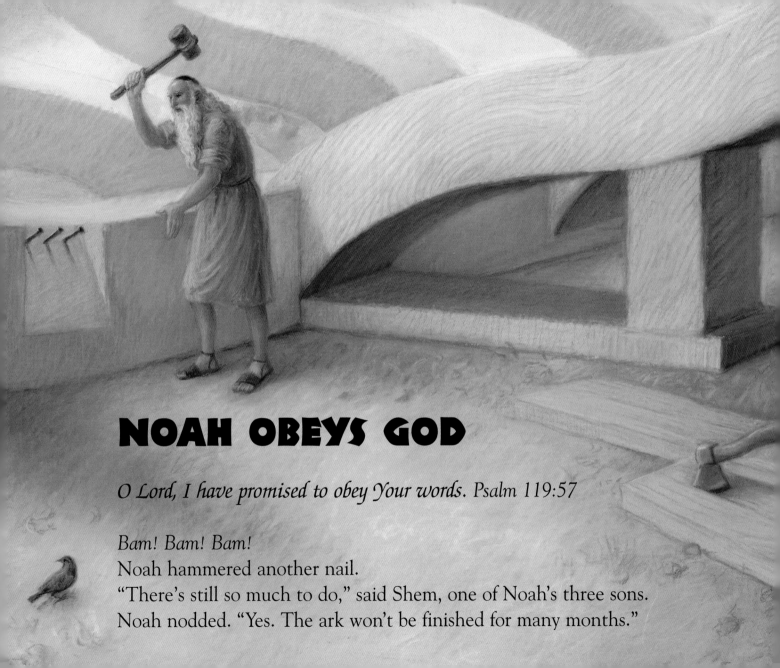

NOAH OBEYS GOD

O Lord, I have promised to obey Your words. Psalm 119:57

Bam! Bam! Bam!
Noah hammered another nail.
"There's still so much to do," said Shem, one of Noah's three sons.
Noah nodded. "Yes. The ark won't be finished for many months."

Noah was right. It would be a long time
before the ark would be ready to float.

"Father, there's one thing I don't understand," said Shem.
"We don't live near water, so why are you building a boat?"

"Each day, I ask the Lord, 'Please lead me so that I may do as You command,'" Noah explained. "When God told me to build a big boat, I obeyed."
"Then my brothers and I shall also do as the Lord commands," said Shem.

NOAH IS PATIENT

A patient man has great understanding. Proverbs 14:29

When the ark was complete, God told Noah to gather the animals.
Two by two, the animals traveled toward the ark. Some of them
moved very slowly, and some of them moved even more slowly.
And others seemed to barely move at all!

Noah's son Ham said, "Can't you hurry up these animals?"
His father said, "Be patient. They move as God wills."
And so they waited and waited while each of the animals took
its turn creeping and crawling onto the big boat.

When the boat was finally full, God sent rain, rain, and more rain. It rained until the ark was tossed on a giant sea.

Finally, the rain stopped.
Noah's third son, Japheth, was tired of being on the ark.
"Each day, I ask the Lord, 'Please lead me so that I may do as You command,'" Noah said. "Because God has said, 'Be patient and stay on this boat,' I will obey."

So they waited and waited until
God told Noah that it was time
to leave the ark.

NOAH THANKS GOD

Give thanks to the Lord. Psalm 105:1

At last, the ark safely reached dry land! When the door opened, all the animals crept and crawled off the ark.
Noah's sons wanted to leave, too, but Noah told them there was something important that they must do first.

Noah said, "Dig up some big, heavy rocks."
His sons obeyed, and Noah said, "Thank you."
Then Noah said, "Find me some wood to build a fire with."
His sons obeyed, and Noah said, "Thank you."

Then Noah said, "Help me stack the rocks to make an altar."
His sons obeyed, and Noah thanked them.

When they were finished, Noah spoke.
"Each day, I ask the Lord, 'Please lead me so that I may do as You command,'" Noah said. "And now the Lord has protected all of us, so let us thank Him."

And so Noah, his sons, and all their families
prayed to God and gave thanks to Him.

Noah had been obedient. He had done what God had asked.
Noah had been patient. He had waited when God told him to wait.
And Noah thanked God for His protection and care.

Because Noah was a good man and had done all these things, God put a rainbow in the sky as a promise that He would never again send so much rain.

For Ashley x

Visit the author's website: www.ericjames.co.uk

Written by Eric James
Illustrated by Sara Sanchez and Darran Holmes
Designed by Nicola Moore

Published by Sourcebooks Jabberwocky, an imprint of Sourcebooks, Inc.
P.O. Box 4410, Naperville, Illinois 60567-4410
(630) 961-3900
Fax: (630) 961-2168
jabberwockykids.com

Date of Production: October 2017
Run Number: HTW_PO250717
Printed and bound in China (IMG)
10 9 8 7 6 5 4 3 2 1

TINY THE Indiana EASTER BUNNY

Written by
Eric James

Illustrated by
Sara Sanchez

sourcebooks
jabberwocky

One bright Easter morning,
while out for a jog,

Tiny hears,

"HELP!
I AM STUCK
IN A LOG."

He scratches his head,
thinking, "Who could that be?
It sounded like Fluff!
I had better go see."

Fluff's in a log
with her feet in the air.
"Hey, Fluff, what on earth
are you doing in there?"

A sad little voice
from an echoey space
says, "I thought this would make
a good egg-hiding place."

"You poor Easter Bunny,"
says Tiny, while giggling.
"I'll get you back out,
just hold tight and stop wriggling!"

Tiny pulls hard,
using all of his might.
He tries and he tries,
but his friend is stuck tight.

"My eggs," sighs poor Fluff.
"Who'll deliver them now?"
"I'll do it," says Tiny.
Fluff laughs and asks,

"How?!"

"Don't worry, dear Fluff.
Leave it all up to me.
I watched you last Easter.
How hard can it be?"

This bunny looks **funny**... Yes, something is **wrong!**

His feet are **too big** and his nose is too **long.**

His skin isn't **furry,** it's wrinkled and rough.

His tail is **too thin,** and it's **NOT** made of fluff.

He's traveled through **South Bend**
and **Evansville** already.
He's all out of puff
and his legs feel unsteady.

The Indiana Bookshop

SWEET TREATS

THE CARDINAL CAFÉ

He **hops**, then he stops,
then he **hops** a bit more,
then he stops all the **hopping...**

and **FLOPS**
to the floor!

Next **West Lafayette**, **Fort Wayne**,
Bloomington too.
There's not much time left
but there's SO MUCH to do!

"Speed up," Marvin squeaks,
"or we'll finish too late!
DiG under that hedge and
HoP over that gate."

This **Conner Prairie** house
has a fence all around.
Poor Tiny tries digging
down into the ground.

But the hole is too small (or his body's too big).
"How odd," Marvin thinks. "I thought bunnies could dig!"

"You do not have whiskers!
You're no good at hopping!
Those ears look quite fake,
and that's no bunny dropping!"

"Aha! Now I've got it!"
He jumps to his toes.
"No bunny is born with a
trunk for a nose!"

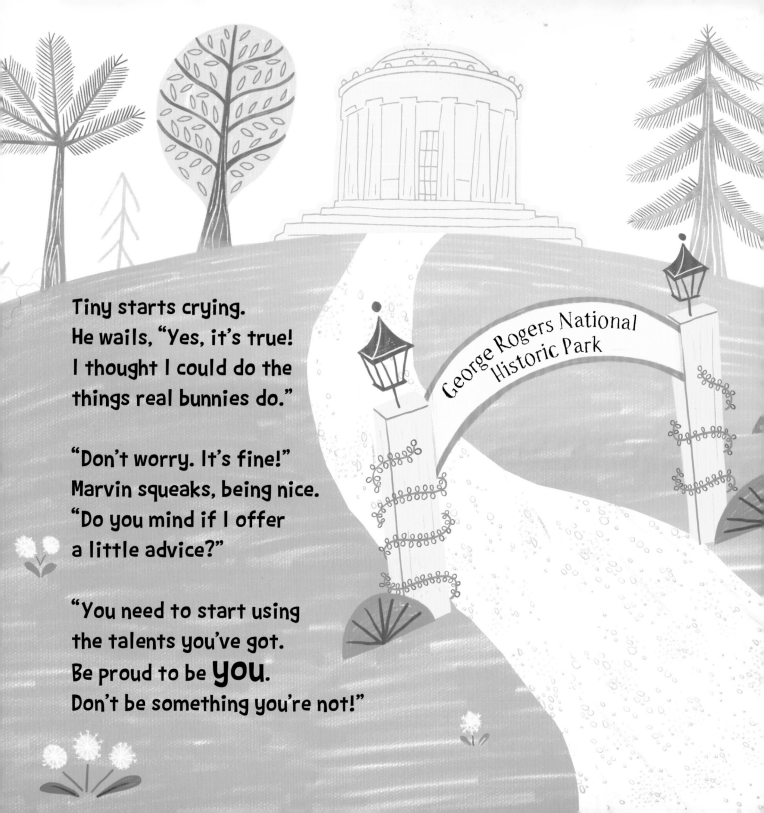

Tiny starts crying.
He wails, "Yes, it's true!
I thought I could do the
things real bunnies do."

"Don't worry. It's fine!"
Marvin squeaks, being nice.
"Do you mind if I offer
a little advice?"

"You need to start using
the talents you've got.
Be proud to be **YOU**.
Don't be something you're not!"

George Rogers National
Historic Park

"What talents?" says Tiny.
"What things can I do?"
He blows his big nose
and then aah...

aaah...

ACHOOOOOO!

"Eureka!" squeaks Marvin
from high in a tree.
"That wonderful,
big trunky nose
is the key!"

"It's strong and it's long.
It can pick things up, too.
It's perfect for seeing
this Easter job through."

"We'll put it to work
just as soon as we can.
Let's head down to **Lafayette**,
test out this plan."

This house has a fence,

and this house has a wall,

but with Tiny's big nose, there's no problem at all!

His long nose lifts up,
reaches over the top,
and he drops an egg down
on the lawn with a

PlOP!

And look at the hole
in this fence...that'll do!
There's room for an egg
and a trunk to fit through.

Now the job seems quite easy. (Well, that's how it goes
when an elephant uses his brains and his nose.)

But daylight is breaking.
The sun starts to rise,
and home after home
stands in front of their eyes.

"I don't think we'll make it,"
squeaks Marvin. "Oh, dear!"
"Hang on," Tiny shouts.
"I've a marvelous idea!"

He sucks all the Easter eggs
into his nose,
and when his trunk's full
he takes aim...then he BLOWS!

Look at those eggs blasting out of his trunk, landing on lawns with a

THUNK!

THUNK!

THUNK!

THUNK!

The basket's soon empty.
"We did it, hooray!
Come on, let's help Fluff.
Oh, I hope she's okay."

At the side
of the pond,
Tiny dips in
his trunk.
He drinks and
he drinks
till the water's
all drunk!

And using
his nose
as a huge
water hose,
he blows
through the log...

Look at Fluff!

UP
she goes!

Happy Easter, Indiana!

How many Easter eggs
are in this picture?